Mrs. McShoogle

Scotland's Second Finest Actress

You couldn't make it up... but she just did.

Jonathan Fortingall

Jonathan Fortingall set himself the challenge of writing two monologues during his daily commutes across London. The first (in your hands) is a lightweight comedy/fantasy and the second (still in the writing) will be a more personal piece. For the past twenty years he has worked in hospices and animal rescue organisations. In an earlier life he edited the *What's On* and *Essential Edinburgh Guides,* and the *Dumfries and Galloway Holiday* and *Children's Guides*.

John Partridge has been a designer and illustrator for many years, more recently specialising in cartoons and caricatures for both commercial and private clients.

Paperback and eBook versions of *Mrs. McShoogle* are available on Amazon.

Mrs. McShoogle

You couldn't make it up... but she just did.

First published in 2020 by Yellow Brick Grove.

Email: yellowbrickgrove@btinternet.com

~ Yellow Brick Grove ~

For my family of friends and
in loving memory of Graeme Clark

"I'm not lost for I know where I am.
But however, where I am may be lost."

A. A. Milne, *Winnie-the-Pooh*

Contents

Foreword

Meet Mrs. McShoogle, 'iconic' actress turned landlady to the stars. Her memoir may be crowded with incident and full of famous faces, but the lady flatters to deceive. Her stories bear no resemblance whatsoever to real life; they are one hundred per cent fiction and fabrication or, to put it bluntly, complete codswallop. Indeed, none of the public figures named herein will recognise one grain of truth in her farcical fibs and fantasies.

This satirical monologue is merely a jape, a jolly josh with a rather sad underbelly, and her 'recollections' do not represent the views or actions of anyone else. It is what it is, as Mrs. McShoogle herself would say in one of her more profound moments.

My special thanks are due to Colin Wakefield for his tip-top support, encouragement and direction, and to John Partridge for providing the witty cover illustration. Finally, a shout-out to Mrs. McShoogle's sometime hero,

Hannah Gordon, and for the wonderful theatre anecdotes shared by actors across dinner tables over the years. They helped to bring Mrs. McShoogle to life, particularly the ones which stretched the truth just a *tad*...

All author's profits from the purchase of this book will be donated to The Born Free Foundation.

Jonathan Fortingall, August 2020.

A Star is Born

You couldn't make it up... but she just did.

[Scottish music plays softly in the background, as Kiki-Jean 'Jeannie' McShoogle reclines on a red tartan sofa in her Strathbogie 'westerly-aspect' front parlour. A wicker chair sits beside a cosy fireplace DL and a diamond leaded window can be seen DR. She is surrounded by hand-embroidered cushions adorned with faces of just some of the characters she has played over the years, including Willy Loman, Veruca Salt and the back end of Clarabelle the Cow. In her late sixties, she retains an air of faded glamour and grandeur. She wears a baby-pink velour tracksuit, matching headband and faux leopard-print mules. As the music fades, she places her glass of vino on the smoked glass table to her right and begins to talk.]

Who would be an actress these days? No one is working. They just sit by the telephone all day eating doughnuts, or worse doing online yoga. I count my blessings to have found fame and fortune in the golden age of Hollywood, 1975 or thereabouts, when a star was still a star, as Frank Carson used to say.

Mrs. McShoogle

I was what they call a child prodigy, belting out Puccini's *O Mio Babbino Caro* while sitting on my potty. You should have heard the cheers when I took my bows, though Mummy told me later they were actually for the poo-poos. She and Daddy were late for a dinner dance at the *[Posh Scots accent] Ethel Pellis Hotel* and I'd been straining away for hours, so the Little Miss Shirley Temple act was beginning to wear a bit thin…

It was Mummy who first spotted the star quality in her only child, or the poor man's Bonnie Langford, as she preferred to call me. You see, Mummy had some experience of the business, having danced at Carnegie Hall… *[Quietly]* in Dunfermline… and could have been the next Judy Garland if Liza Minnelli hadn't had an unfair advantage. What's the point in being *nouveau riche* if we don't exploit the girl, she used to shout at poor Daddy, when he pleaded with her just to let me enjoy my childhood.

You couldn't make it up… but she just did.

Every day after playgroup she would march me to the highly regarded Monica Glen School of Drama and Car Maintenance for my Theatres of Modernity class, and it wasn't long before I made my stage *day-boo* in their Christmas production, *Mary and Joseph: Put a Ring on It*, exquisitely directed by local drug baron, Big Tam Mouskouri. I played the innkeeper's wife, such a complex character for one so young. How could a wifey who works in the service industry heartlessly turn away a heavily pregnant woman? And just before Christmas!

The strain of playing such a wretched creature got to me in the end and I had the most dreadful stage fright on opening night, boking up last night's kebab all down my costume. My understudy managed to sponge most of it off in the wings, but the stench was something awful. You should have heard the gagging from the front row when I entered stage left. Still, my hard work paid off when I received a rave review from Kate Adie, of all people, in *Scaffolders' Monthly*.

Kiki-Jean is a mere four years old, she wrote, but she is utterly perfect in the role of this prize bitch. So real was her performance one wonders if she was acting at all. The cheeky besom! I'll give her a war zone if I ever run into her…

By the time I graduated from Strathbogie High School I was big in Tomintoul, but this didn't half incur the wrath of my grubby little form master, Mr. Vainglory. He would sit there, huge belly spilling over his far too short kilt, and tell me I should seriously consider a career in retail. Retail! Kiki-Jean Mankini, he said, do you have an interest in shoes? Well, I assumed the old pervert had some weird foot fetish, so I swung my thigh-length boots under the desk and said, no, Mr. Vain, none whatsoever. Oh, that is a shame, he told me, as you've just passed up a possible interview with Clarks Shoes in the High Street. The perfect career for a young lady of your intellect. Ruddy cheek, I said, I am an actress. I am going to Hollywood. You are going to Barlinnie, he replied, rather unhelpfully, I felt, so I stood up, stubbed out my ciggie on his bald patch, and told him, *nichi problemi*, we actors love a captive audience. I'll entertain the prisoners with my *Habeas Corpus*. Well, that shut him up, didn't it! Call yourself a teacher when you can't speak a word of Latin?

Our local minister, Reverend Toby Sparkle, was much more supportive. He came to see me in the WI production of *Equus* and begged me afterwards to join St. Lolita's Church Choir. I tried to explain that hymns don't move me in the same way as, say, *Cotton Eye Joe*, but he won me over when he said the next choral concert would be a selection of works by Marc Almond. It turned out Toby Sparkle was a very progressive young minister, with his *I've Never Been to Me* T-shirt and penis piercings. As a teen I always wanted a tattoo exactly like his but thank God I dodged that bullet. Who needs a naked Terry Wogan straddling a motorbike on their forearm in 2020? Mummy used to say, your nice young minister is something of a pin-up with the old dears at McCarthy & Stone. She tried to tell them they were barking up the wrong tree, but they just didn't get *Tainted Love*, bless them.

It was my beloved cousin, Bobbly-Sue, who accompanied me to London to follow my dream of becoming a professional actress. On our first night in the big city she said, let's go and see some *real* theatre, as opposed to the Strathbogie Rep. variety. We must have spent hours poring over the reviews. There were comedies, tragedies, musicals, even Shakespeare, who never really caught on north of the border, but we finally chose something called *The Chippendales*.

I was so thankful we did, when the following day at my audition for drama school Prunella Scales asked me to give a critique of the last play I'd seen. Talk about a gift. I must have blethered on for hours about each character... the cop, the cowboy and the Roman Emperor, played by someone called

You couldn't make it up… but she just did.

Hunky Hans in a dental floss thong. Prunella said it sounded marvellous and she and Timothy simply must go, and then invited me to give my audition speech. And can I be frank, she said, I'm buggered if I'll sit through one more *wherefore art thou*. Surprise me, Kiki-Jean Mankini. Surprise me! Well, I think you're going to like this, I said, as I whipped off my bra and put in my false teeth. For tonight, Pru, I am going to be… Sybil Fawlty! *[Sybil Fawlty's voice]* Oh, I *know*!

There I was, waiting for her to say, darling, you're even better at me than I am, but it was all a bit awkward as I got nothing. Zippo! I still don't know how I got through my speech, the moving scene when Sybil opens up to some passing Lothario about her mother's morbid fears, but even when I'd finished, she just sat there staring at me as if she was in shock or something. I heard later she wanted to sue, but when Bob the Street Cat turned down their offer and went to RADA instead, she was overruled and six weeks later there I was, standing on the steps of the prestigious Peggy Mountview Theatre School!

I always said the wrong Peggy got the damehood. Ashcroft was fine in the right role but could never have carried a sitcom. Peggy Mount was an inspiration and helped to keep her young *protégés'* feet on the ground. You there in the tiara, she would shout at me, don't come crying to me when you're just another out of work actor on a park bench pretending to read Beckett. But she meant it in a *caring* way…

It was the same with our singing teacher, Pierce Brosnan, who trained us only to use the notes la, ti, do. Ignore the rest, he said, I always do. It will save on warm-up time, it's all you'll ever need for *Take That Look Off Your Face* and using the others is simply vulgar and attention-seeking. But it was our esteemed patron, Larry Olivier, who shared with us the secret of becoming a truly great actor. *[Loud whisper, Larry Olivier's voice]* Try not to talk over the other actors, darlings, he would say. Let them finish their lines before you start yours. Well, talk about genius! You could have heard a pin drop.

After that, I always tried to let my fellow actors get their sentences out first, although it was more of a life sentence waiting for Keira Knightley to finally finish emoting. I once polished off a whole packet of Cheesy Wotsits waiting for her to get through Lady Macbeth's *Hands That Do Dishes* speech. Next thing, the director's shouting, Cut! I whispered to Keira, and they say actors are divas... Then I had it out with him. Is there a problem, Mr. Tarantino? The problem is, he said, a lady-in-waiting would not be munching on pre-packaged savoury snacks in Elizabethan times. What, not even Pringles, I protested? But he had already flounced off. I'm sure that can't be right. I'd spent a good half hour in Lesmahagow Library researching my role as serving wench open-bracket-brunette-close-bracket and not one historian mentioned a shortage of crisps.

It was such an honour when our period movement tutors voted me the student most likely to appear in *Hi-De-Hi!*, but it didn't half unleash the jealous rage of my fellow drama students. Even my lovely Scottish accent was fair game. Try that again in English, they would say, we didn't understand a word of it! Well, *Jings, Crivens, Help Ma Boab*, I told them, *I am fair scunnert wi' yis bunch ae sleekit, cow'rin, tim'rous beasties.* Look at all the outstanding actors Scotland has given to the world over the years. There's me. Robbie Coltrane. Wasn't he wonderful in *Nuns on the Run*? Ronnie Corbett, of course. James Naughtie. And Audrey and Katharine Hepburn's sister... the footballer. You know, the one with the home perm. Dee Hepburn! That's her. And, oh... too many to mention!

You couldn't make it up… but she just did.

Superstar

One never forgets one's first appearance in the West End. I was playing a young Cleo Laine in *The Shabbadoodleyweewee Affair* and on opening night I looked up at the poster outside the Gaiety and finally found my name, thirteen below Moira Stuart. Jeannie Mankini, you've only gone and made it, I screamed, scaring the living daylights out of some passing Japanese tourists. And I felt that same buzz of excitement every performance during the entire run. They truly were two and a half of the best weeks of my life.

But as one door closed another opened, when I was cast opposite Ralph Richardson, Celia Johnson and Margaret Leighton in Ken Russell's classic thriller, *Skinnydippin'*. Not one, but three icons of British cinema! Sadly, I didn't actually meet any of them as I was only on set for one day, but my role as skinnydippin' water polo girl number four was integral to the plot. Then something devastating happened. The director cut my scene completely! He must have had some kind of breakdown, there's no other explanation, but it was a cruel blow, nonetheless. I'd told everyone about me and my pals, Celia, Ralph and Margaret, and it was too late now. Mummy and Daddy had booked the sleeper train *fae* Ecclefechan for the premiere and I wasn't even in the bloody thing.

Thank God, the producers were very kind and on the night me and the other axed water polo girlies were allowed up on stage to join the cast. The only thing was they made us stand in the third row so no one in the audience could see us. I put up with it for a few minutes, then tapped Denholm Elliott on the shoulder and promised to sort out his dandruff if he'd budge up a bit. I managed to squeeze in between him and Lynda Bellingham and I could see the audience a lot better from there. I felt for the three stars in the front row, though. They looked so lonely out there on their own, so I took one more step forward and found myself between Celia Johnson and Margaret

Leighton! Truth be told, they looked a bit nonplussed to see me, but instinct took over and I grabbed their hands, shouted, we love you all to the audience, and took a bow.

Well, before you could say, move over darling, the audience rose to their feet and Celia, Margaret and Ralph found themselves bobbing up and down with me. I must have bowed seven times as the adrenaline just kept pumping! I'd dreamt of this moment and I never wanted it to end. Thankfully, Celia spotted that poor old Ralph was on the verge of collapse, so she let go of his hand and some kind soul brought him a chair, but we three iconic actresses just kept on going. I could hear Margaret shouting in my ear, cut it out, cut it out you bitch as I bowed over and over, but I shouted back, feel the love, Maggie! Feel the love!

My parents were beaming with pride, but they were a tad puzzled after the film had finished. Were you actually *in* it, Mummy asked? You didn't see me, I said? No, Daddy said, we kept thinking you must be in the next scene, but you never were. Oh, you missed me, I assured him, I was the one who looked like Lynda Bellingham. But I thought that *was* Lynda Bellingham, Mummy said. No, that was me done up to look like her, I said, it's called acting. I wasn't sure if they'd buy it, but I needn't have worried, they'd have believed I was Ralph Richardson, they were so proud. You're an even better actress than we thought, they said, which was so beautiful to hear!

It was just a shame that once Celia and Margaret pulled me off to the side of the stage, a couple of security guards ushered me out through a different exit to the rest of the cast. We never did manage to find a way into the after-show party, but we hung around outside to say goodnight. Mummy heard Celia muttering something under her breath about *that Z-list psycho* as she hurried past. She must have been referring to Margaret Leighton.

You can guess who was splashed all over the front pages in the morning! *Stars' Fury as Deranged Scottish Extra Storms Stage* screamed the headlines. I needed a whole new scrapbook for my press cuttings, but you can imagine my potty mouth when I saw myself described as an *extra*. My darling agent, Champion Soames of Cast-off Casting, was very reassuring, however, and said the phone had been ringing off the hook all day. It was very gratifying, I must say, and we sat down together and sifted through the offers. In the end we ruled out the Shopping Channel, which left us with an impossible decision… a juicy run on Broadway or the lead in a movie!

The movie was a low-budget affair called *Totally Hot Stuff*, being filmed by a group of randy students at the Anglia Ruskin University Halls of Residence. All good so far, but Champion had real concerns about the film's finances. How would he get his fifteen per cent if the boys had already spent their student loans? And I had to bring my own sandwiches. No, the road ahead was clear. Kiki-Jean Mankini was on her way to Broadway! Well, off-Broadway, truth to tell, so far off-Broadway it's in Connecticut, Jane Fonda said. But what an honour to play opposite Dame Maggie Smith in a Hispanic production of *Trafford Tanzi*.

An honour and a great responsibility on my slender shoulders. By the time my Aeroflot flight touched down at JFK, I was cacking myself, I don't mind telling you, so it was such a nice surprise to arrive at my digs and find I was sharing with my old friends, The Krankies. They were in town working as Grace Jones' backing dancers, and after their show Wee Jimmy would grab his hula hoop and we would hot trot it down to Studio 54 and hang out with anyone who was anyone in NYC. Warren Beatty, Salvador Dali, Cheryl Baker, they just couldn't get enough of the wee lassies in their tartan pinafores! One minute Andy Warhol and I were *geein' it laldy* to *Oops Upside Your Head* and the next lovely old Stevie Nicks was twirling Wee

Jimmy round and round the dancefloor, shrouded in veils and high as a kite, wailing pigs in space, pigs in space! Bianca Jagger said it was the funniest thing she'd ever seen. And you've seen Mick naked, I said. Oh, we laughed!

But behind all the glitz and the glamour, no one could have predicted the heartbreak of my play being taken off after opening night, or during the *interval* of opening night, as *The New York Times* enjoyed putting in capitals on their front page. The reviews were so offensive that I demanded retractions, but Dame Maggie just wanted to get home to her budgies. This wrestling malarkey isn't for me, darling, she said, from now on I'll stick to Pilates. At our first night-cum-wrap party, I tried to get her to open up to me, but she couldn't do it. I'm sorry, Kira-Jane, she said, magnificent Maggie is a maudlin Maggie tonight. Even national treasures need a night off occasionally. I felt myself welling up and Wee Jimmy was in pieces, so we left her cutting her toenails and said we really must pop to the powder room. And that's when it happened…

There I was, sitting on the loo, thinking if it doesn't happen tonight it never will, when who knocks on the door but Richard Burton! I invited him in for a nightcap, but you can imagine my surprise when he knelt down, looked at me with those bewitching grey-green eyes of his and slurred, *Delores, Delores…* But I'm Kiki-Jean, I said, a mite confused, Kiki-Jean Mankini, charmed I'm sure. But it was to no avail. *Delores*, he burped, I must talk to you, man to woman, great actor to… *you.* It's a tough business out there, but don't let them break you. You are delicious, darling. *Delicious.* Never forget it. And I haven't! In fact, I often sit here and wonder what might have been if Liz Taylor hadn't tapped on the door and asked to borrow some bog roll. Not the first thing you'd expect to come out of Cleopatra's mouth, but no one likes to be caught short…

Lone Star State of Mind

You couldn't make it up… but she just did.

It was after my moving portrayal of Babette Plechette, the demonic lollipop lady in *Crimewatch on Ice,* that my fame began to take its toll on poor Mummy and Daddy. They couldn't even walk round the Strathbogie Co-op without petty, spiteful comments. We saw your Jeannie on telly. Shame about the terrible reviews. I've read they're stopping that show of hers. Isn't she married yet? Doesn't she want to have a family? I have six beautiful grandchildren myself. That la-di-da lifestyle is all well and good, but Shakespeare won't keep you warm at night. You wouldn't believe what they had to put up with, but Mummy was an absolute gem. She would smile serenely and say, we are very proud of our Jeannie, please send our regards to your grandchildren. Then she'd tell them to *feck* right off and she and Daddy would go and buy their Stella Artois in peace.

I know how Sheena Easton must have felt when she returned home to Glasgow an American superstar. The way those jealous young oiks threw beer bottles at her was a disgrace. Fair enough, that drippy ballad she was warbling didn't do anyone any favours, but we're talking about a friend of Prince here. And things went from bad to worse when I started to be offered bit parts on number two tours! I'd sit for hours reading the so-called script, yellow highlighter in hand, trying to find my character, but I really didn't fancy hanging around backstage for two hours just to say *is that still or sparkling, madam?*

Lovely Bill Kenwright was desperate to hire me, but I said, Bill, you only pay enough for Premier Inns and I'm just not that kind of girl. I had supper with him recently and we had a good old chinwag. As we were leaving, I sent my love to Jenny Agutter and he looked at me and said, I don't know Jenny Agutter. I laughed and said, you silly man, you've lived with her for decades! No, I live with Jenny Seagrove, he said. Oh, same difference, I said. How we laughed! The fact is, I was destined to be one of the greats, but

You couldn't make it up… but she just did.

I got tired of waiting around for someone else to notice it. Sure, I could have understudied, but I wasn't willing to play second fiddle to Glenda Jackson. She's a competent actress. I'm a competent actress. Why would one get the bouquets while the other flicks through *Take a Break* in the dressing room?

I blame those hideous casting directors; they kept offering my roles to Helen Mirren of all people. Every time I turned up for a casting, there she was. Looking gorgeous, I must say, but so smug in that effortlessly chic biker's jacket. I mean, anyone can imitate the Queen. Kenny Everett did it. Heavens to Betsy, Janet Brown did it every Saturday night on telly for years.

I can't bear to think of the number of times I lost out on the perfect role to someone who, when it came to it, couldn't quite pull it off. It got to the point I could not bring myself to watch Meryl Streep. I am a huge admirer of her chameleon-like ability to change her hairstyle, but oh, I wish she'd worked harder on those accents.

To the outside world I was a hugely successful actress, desired by men and admired by women everywhere and, in public at least, I never fell short of perfection. But in private it was a different story and I began to feel like Jane McDonald after someone had let the air out. Finally, the day came when I was admiring myself in the hall mirror and it hit me. Jeannie Mankini, there simply aren't enough parts for an actress as beautiful as you. And there was no way I was making myself look unattractive just for an acting role.

It didn't help that at the time I was schlepping up and down to the Space Hopper Theatre, Sunderland, to play a glamorous library assistant in a terrible, terrible Tom Stoppard. I spent half the time on stage stamping books and the other half getting jiggy with Nigel Havers in a Ford Cortina. No actor should have to face that.

You couldn't make it up… but she just did.

Not with Nigel Havers. I managed to stagger through the rest of the run, then took myself off to Southwold for a mini-break with my dear friend, Barbra Streisand. Barbra and I talked and talked, and it turned out we were at very similar stages in our careers. She had recently recorded a song with Donna Summer and was about to open at Caesars Palace and I'd just finished a walk-on in *The Bill* and was the new face of Fleshcreep antifungal cream.

That weekend we both made brave decisions. Barbra would clone her alpaca and record a yodelling concept album and I would walk away from acting while at the peak of my career. It was time for me to give something back. I would open the most sumptuous theatrical digs in the business! Babs and I toasted new dimensions, personal and professional, and then trotted off to the local rep. to see some interminably awful thriller. She turned to me at the interval and said, it's enough to make me give up acting too. What a thought! Can you imagine, if she hadn't changed her mind when she returned to LA, none of us would have had the pleasure of *Little Fockers*…

I waved her off in her Bubble car with strict instructions to avoid the A12 and caught the train back to swinging London… well, it was swinging up Richard and Judy's end of town *anyhoo*… and that evening, as I was drooling over Joe McFadden in *Take the High Road*, it came to me. My theatrical digs would be in my hometown and the theatre capital of Scotland, Strathbogie! I would open my heart and my home to the poor, the needy and the degenerate… my fellow actors.

I say *my* home, but the truth is Mummy and Daddy were very generous. I simply called them up and explained the situation and they immediately offered to move out of the family home they'd loved for forty years into a vintage two-berth caravan I picked up at the dump and parked in the driveway. It was bitter out there in the winter, but they always looked forward to a nice warming cuppa

You couldn't make it up... but she just did.

each morning in my... *their* kitchen, may they rest in peace and bricks and mortar. Truth is, I would have offered them a room in the house if there was the space, but how would I manage without the extra bunk beds if the Spice Girls came to stay? You couldn't put any of them in the same room. They'd kill each other! *Zig-a-zig-ah*, indeed. It's hardly Bob Dylan, is it?

Starman

You couldn't make it up… but she just did.

I think you'd like the peace and quiet of Strathbogie. It's what they call a handsome town, with lots of craggy period features… think Jude Law after he hit forty… but once I'd unpacked my panto cosies and sat down to admire the view I began to wonder if this whole *Escape to the Country* thing wasn't a tad overrated. That first winter was never-ending, until one *dreich* February afternoon I was sitting in the Toot-Toot Tea Room at Strathbogie Railway Station, when who should walk in but my future, errant husband, Maurice McShoogle. I can still see him standing there, legs akimbo, asking if he could squeeze his rugby player thighs onto the stool beside me. They're the biggest in central Scotland, he said, as I sipped on my Bovril. Are they really, I replied, thinking, I don't remember that line in *Brief Encounter?*

I'm in the business, I said, once we got the formalities out of the way, but he seemed to find this hilarious and said he wasn't paying for it if that was what I meant. I was raging, I can tell you, but before I could enlighten the Neanderthal, he mentioned he was a fireman. For some reason that really impressed me. I'm not sure why, it may have had something to do with my guttering, but from then on, I began to see him in a whole new light. You see, poor Maurice was brought up in a strict, puritanical household on the Isle of Bahookie, so it wasn't all his fault. I'm a bit of a livewire, but he wasn't much of a talker or a toucher, if you know what I'm saying. I'm a great admirer of Mother Nature, but what *was* she thinking when she decided to allow a straight man and a straight woman to procreate? We girlies need a woman's mind in a man's body, someone like Tom Hardy for example, but try as I might I could not find Maurice's hidden depths.

In the end, I resorted to playing *Islands in the Stream* over and over, but even that didn't turn him into a freethinker. I blamed his mother, old Tammy Baker. She didn't approve of her son dating an actress. I can still see that pinched face, swathed in shawls, screaming at me for hanging my Victoria's Secrets out to dry on a Sunday. The Devil will have you, she shouted. He already has, love, I shouted back.

Maurice and I got married after a couple of weeks, which we felt was ample time to get to know each other and plan a wedding for about a hundred guests, but with hindsight it may have been a teensy bit premature. I blame all the improvisation at drama school. It has left me hopelessly spontaneous, and before you could say, the gift list is at Jenners, I was walking down the aisle as Mrs. Maurice McShoogle!

It really was the most glorious day. The ceremony was held on a deserted beach in Scotland's Hawaii, Millport. It was so romantic, despite the hailstones and gale-force winds, and the RNLI were super-helpful when our photographer managed to get herself swept out to sea. Maurice was all for wading in to save her, but I said not to bother, as Auntie Sookie and Uncle Juan had found a buy-one-get-one-free deal on disposable cameras so we'd manage.

Later, we retired to the celebrity Little Chef at the Ardrossan Service Station for a slap-up meal and the all-important speeches. Darling Daddy brought the house down when he thanked Maurice for giving me a go and reassured him there would be no hard feelings if he met someone better! But I'm sorry to say Maurice spectacularly failed to embrace the spirit of the occasion. The filthy fireman humour was neither here nor there, but he lost us completely with his ruminations on Jean-Paul Sartre's *Existentialism and the Alpha Male*. By the time he thanked his ex-girlfriend, Ryvita, for helping to make him a man, he was getting on my wick, so I interrupted to ask if it was Ryvita who gave him the little social disease which made his groin that peculiar colour? I gave her a little wave to show there were no hard feelings, and he rather lost his thread and sat down shortly afterwards, much to everyone's relief.

You couldn't make it up… but she just did.

Thankfully, *The People's Friend* picked up the tab for the whole shebang as I had arranged a lucrative deal for exclusive access and photos on the condition we got some famous faces along. That wasn't difficult as my dress was by Su Pollard, electric pink with plastic accessories, and my flower girls, Debbie McGee and a very young Kimberley from Girls Aloud, looked stunning in lime and tangerine taffeta. But *The People's Friend* insisted we up the celebrity quota by inviting Rick Astley and Helena Bonham Carter, even though we'd never met them in our lives!

Rick was in the middle of his wilderness years, bless him, so he jumped at the chance of a hot meal, but Helena was much harder to pin down, with all sorts of demands being faxed across by her people. In the end I won her over by saying Dame Dawn French was coming. On the day she kept pestering me, saying, where's the Dame, where is she? So, in the end I took her hand and led her over to Tony, my outrageous drag queen friend.

Dame Dawn, Helena... Helena, Dame Dawn, I said, and left them to it. Well, she never twigged the whole evening. Every time I passed them, I could hear her prattling on about *The Vicar of Dibley* changing her life. Tony told me later he'd never heard of Helena Bonham Carter and he thought he'd been talking to another rather over-the-top drag queen all night!

But as Maurice and I waved cheery-bye to our family and friends we faced the same problem as so many newlyweds... with the wedding over, we had bugger all left to talk about. I had seen the signs on our third date, when we had a series of explosive rows trying to choose our first dance of the evening. He wanted *You're So Vain*. He said it reminded him of me, which was sweet, but I got my way, *naturellement*, and chose Susan Boyle's delightful cover of *Love Will Tear Us Apart*.

And don't believe the hype about the so-called honeymoon period. Even on our wedding night, after we returned to the Hotel Brigadoon, Maurice started asking for some very strange things in bed. I told him, I was not dressing up as Carmen Miranda, nor was I prepared to do *Riverdance* at double speed just to spice up a failing honeymoon. You know what he said? A man has his needs! Well, you claim to be a whiz at Do It Yourself, I told him. He didn't like that, did he, and threatened to divide up the wedding presents right there and then. I wouldn't have minded, but he said the Capodimonte was mine and he'd cop the rest!

It wasn't a great start and, so much for sacred vows, five weeks later… five weeks, I tell you… he's only flaunting his thighs to Britney Spears' sister-in-law, Broccoli. She seemed like such a sweet young thing when she arrived to stay and I rather took her under my wing, even pretending to like Britney's music. That took all my play-it-for-real tips from Dickie Attenborough, I can tell you, but I knew something was up when she started asking for extra oranges and bananas in her fruit bowl. She could not get enough fruit, until finally it hit me… he'd found his Carmen Miranda!

I had it out with the pair of them that evening, after Laurence Fox had finally got bored of the sound of his own voice, and she was at least contrite. Oops, I did it again, she said, and burst into tears. As for Maurice, he didn't say anything. He just grabbed a clean pair of Y-fronts and his toolbox and moved in with his mate, Pongo. I was in pieces. I'd given him my heart, and all those Viennettas, and this was how he repaid me. I didn't leave the house for days, I just sat there, staring at the telly. I sat through an entire episode of *The Jewel in the Crown* one evening. That's how bad it got.

Maurice and I only met as a married couple once or twice after that, court appearances and on *The Jeremy Kyle Show*, that kind of thing, then I heard he had met someone else. Another actress! Can you believe it? Name of Cyndi-Lou Redgrave. You won't have heard of her. She's not in *Spotlight*, I looked. Turns out Cyndi-Lou Redgrave isn't even her real name. It's Kelly Bung, but she wanted everyone to think she was one of the Redgraves! Vanessa was furious when I told her. I have enough bloody Redgraves to compete with without another one, she said.

Maurice and I had talked about having children and building an acting dynasty, but the truth is we couldn't be fagged. All that extra workload and I had my darling cats, Kate O'Mara and Sidney Poitier, to think of. They would have hated the inconvenience and the noise. I've always had a strict *No Children* rule in the house, apart from once, when, as a special favour to Raisa Gorbachev, I allowed the cast of *The Famous Five* to stay. They were polite enough kids to have around but, Gordon Bennett, they took the *Stanislavski* method so seriously. I had to put my foot down when they went round to the neat little council estate behind me and flashed their torches through the windows shouting, you're working class and up to no good. I told them, it really isn't healthy to live and breathe a dramatic role 24/7. Look at poor Daniel Day-Lewis, not to mention Martine McCutcheon. But did they listen? Did they *Humperdinck*. After a couple of days, I ended up putting sleeping pills in their Ready Brek just to try and keep the noise down.

One night Dick and George asked me, Mrs. McShoogle, Mrs. McShoogle, can we have a lager with our meal instead of ginger pop? Well, I don't remember The Famous Five drinking lager, I said, but they assured me they did. You must be thinking of The Secret Seven, said Dick, they were teetotal. Mm, how old are you, I asked? Thirteen, they said. Oh, what the hell, I said, a couple of cans won't do any harm, and they seemed to know their Foster's from their Budweiser. Well, you can guess the rest. Years later I looked them up on IMDb, which happens to give their dates of birth. Turns out they were only nine at the time. Nine! You've got to laugh!

You couldn't make it up… but she just did.

I Lost My Heart to a Starship Trooper

People are constantly asking me, Kiki-Jean, who was your favourite guest, but I always say, how can I choose? Sir Elton John kept on at me, am I your favourite, Kiki-Jean? Am I? Please say it's me and not Diana Rigg. But God love him, and I do, I think it would have to be Benedict Cumberbatch. That man's neck is exquisite. One evening I bent over to offer him a doily and had this overpowering urge to bite it, but he got up to make himself an Angel Delight just in time. He's *nowt* from the front, of course, but walk round the back and oh, my giddy aunt…

When he left, I could not bring myself to wash his bath towel. I know what you're thinking, but I simply couldn't do it. Zoë Wanamaker said to me, sell it on eBay, Kiki-Jean, you'll make a fortune, but I said, no, Zoë, tawdry, Zoë. In the end, I added it to my little theatrical museum in the back hall. There are all sorts of memorabilia on display. Old Strathbogie programmes, a G-string worn by Simon Russell Beale I found inside his Gideon Bible, and now Benedict's used towel. I hung it up and put a wee plaque beside it with an arrow showing the imprint of his little bubble butt. I once got up in the middle of the night to go to the bathroom and caught Bob Hoskins having a good sniff of it. He was mortified, went scarlet red and said, *[Cockney accent]* honest, Kiki-Jean, I was just drying my face. I smiled at him and said, of course you were, Bob, you enjoy yourself, but please don't block my rear passage. It's a fire hazard.

Welcoming Britain's *greatest* living actor to my humble home was an honour I could never have expected, and Hannah Gordon did not disappoint. That woman could play any role, any gender, any age. Whoever could forget her tender performances in *Upstairs, Downstairs* and *Watercolour Challenge*? We bonded immediately, two fine Scots actresses and two strong yet vulnerable women, and when she left, she held on to me with tears in her eyes. Thank you, Katie-Joan, she said, we will always be friends. I haven't heard from her since, but no doubt she's been busy, shopping in Safeway and things.

You'll be surprised to hear that some of my guests take advantage of my good nature. I was so warm and welcoming to Golden Girl Bea Arthur when she flew in to do the Whisky Trail. I loved your sitcom, I said. Thank you, she said. Donald Sinden was so funny in it, I said. Donald Sinden wasn't in it, she said. Well, the last time I looked he was, I said, he was your butler! That wasn't me, she said. Oh, who can it have been, I said? Elaine Stritch, she said. Oh, I love Elaine Stritch, I said, she's so funny. I'm Bea Arthur, she said. Of course, you are, dearie, I said, and weren't you wonderful in *Rising Damp*? I wasn't in that either, she said. Well, who the blazes was, I said? Frances de la Tour, she said. Oh, I love Frankie, I said, she's so talented! I could tell she was now getting seriously p'd off and I thought, for God's sake, Jeannie, think! What was this blasted woman in? Then I remembered reading how much she loathed lovely old Betty White. At last, something to go on. You were wonderful in *The Mary Tyler Moore Show*, I said. *[Shouts]* I wasn't in *The Mary Tyler Moore Show*, she said, I was the star of *The Golden Girls*. Of course, you were, dearie, I said, not particularly liking her tone. And very good you were too. But didn't Betty White win the Emmy?

And don't get me started on those musical theatre types. Where the hell is the off button? Look at me, Kiki-Jean, I can do the splits! No, look at *me*, Kiki-Jean, I can do a cartwheel! Well, after half an hour of *I'm Gonna Live Forever* I had to have it out with Olly Murs. Heavens to Murgatroyd, knock it off, I said, you're nearly forty. Then the tears. Please don't shout at me, Kiki-Jean, I'm an all-round entertainer and former Rear of the Year. And so is Germaine Greer, I said, and look where it got her.

I blame Andrew Lloyd Webber myself. I adore that man, but I had to ask, Andy, why do you keep writing those dreary musicals with only one decent song that is sung over and over again? Everyone in the audience is sitting there, praying to God for something... *anything* to happen. And to think he wrote *Pie Jesu* for that Sarah Brightman. When she played me the demo I said, sweetie, it's exquisite but it's simply crying out for a disco remix. We're talking *I Lost My Heart to a Starship Trooper* here, but did she listen? Did she *Bacharach*. And while Michael Ball may be every octogenarian's fantasy, why must he act out every word in *Love Changes Everything* like Lionel Blair on heat? We know where our hands and faces are, laddie! I ended up turning to the lady next to me and asking her, do you think he's drunk? No, just cheesy, she said.

But did you know Barbara Dickson was the first leading lady in *Blood Brothers*? It's true. Before all those greedy Nolan Sisters got their paws on it. When she turned up on my doorstep I was lost for words. Ye gods, you are ageing gracefully, I said, that perm is timeless. And Maurice will be fair made up as he is a huge fan of your little folk ditties about living in a caravan in January and February. She apologised for not booking in advance and asked if I had room for a little one. Oh, did you bring Elaine Paige, I said, pretending to search in her handbag? No, really, I said, you are welcome to my side-facing single if you don't mind nylon sheets.

Maurice was like a love-struck teenager when he got home from his shift and saw Barbara levitating in the dinette. I would have trimmed my nasal hair if I'd known, he said! She gave him such a big hug and graciously thanked him for being a fan. He held on to her tightly and said, can I slip something welcoming into your hand, Barbic? Well, she looked a bit taken aback to say the least, but he blushed something awful and said, I meant a drink, Barbie! Honest, I did! How we laughed! Oh, I miss that man. Yes, I know, he's ignorant, two-timing trash, but there's a time and a place for everything. You know what I mean?

Not that I have a minute to myself. It's a full-time commitment being, and I quote from *The Stage, the oldest and dampest theatrical digs in Strathbogie*. I pride myself on offering every home comfort to my actors. They're away from the wife and kids, often for a whole summer season, but at least they can enjoy the glorious Highland scenery and some nice horny flings with other members of the company. I'll never forget the sight of Burt Reynolds tiptoeing out of Burt Lancaster's room in a negligee. So, that's what they mean by a Burt in the hand, I shouted after him. Didn't he laugh!

For some, though, the strain is too much. I came down one morning to find darling Emma Thompson sobbing in that wicker chair. She was overdoing it, of course, eight shows a week in Cameron Mackintosh's *New Balls Please – the Musical*, playing a deeply disturbed character. The critics said it was the best portrayal of Sue Barker they'd ever seen. It was heartbreaking to see Em sitting there, rocking back and forth, clutching her

You couldn't make it up… but she just did.

Golden Globe to her chest and wailing, anyone for tennis, anyone for tennis? I said to her, I understand, lassie, for I have been there. *Doc Martin* left me traumatised for months. But try and look on the bright side. Have you *seen* that Kenneth Branagh recently?

Mrs. McShoogle

Starry, Starry Night

You couldn't make it up... but she just did.

I was a great admirer of the late Princess of Wales, or DiDi, as she insisted on me calling her. I met her when she came to open the new shortbread factory on the Strathbogie Industrial Estate. I think I stood out because of my directness. I curtseyed, a nice slow, deep one like Mrs. Thatcher gave to the Queen, only mine wasn't sarcastic, and asked her straight, what are *you* doing here? You're more of a Fondant Fancy kind of girl. And she had to cover her mouth she was laughing so much! So, I lowered my voice, more serious like, and said, you should be with that nice George Michael. And Cliff Richard should be with Olivia Newton-John, but that's another story.

Next thing, I saw the tears in her eyes and I thought, Jeannie, you've really gone and done it now, she'll set Fergie on you, but no, she stepped forward and hugged me and whispered in my ear that she could never be with George Michael because he was gay! Don't be ridiculous, dearie, I said, haven't you heard the lyrics to *Young Guns (Go for It)*?

But she smiled and said, don't be fooled by all that *Wham! Bam! I am a Man!* stuff. Well, can you imagine? I had so many questions. George? Gay? What about the shuttlecocks? Did Pepsi and Shirley know?

Bless her, DiDi must have given me a rave review at the Palace, as the following spring who should call but Princess Margaret looking to book a spa break. Well, I didn't think you'd be working, I said, but I'm fully booked, and even if I had a room, I am a strictly *No Smoking* establishment. Cue a chilly silence and a sharp intake of breath somewhere in Kensington. Joan Collins was allowed to smoke, came the retort, why can't I? Because she's Joan Collins, I said. *[Shouts]* And I'm Princess Margaret, came the voice down the line. Means nothing to me, love, I said, and with that I sent my regards to Tony Armstrong-Jones and replaced the receiver. Tony took a stunning photo of me when I was just starting out as an actress. Topless, but very tasteful, on a parky day at the Oban ferry terminal.

You couldn't make it up… but she just did.

I'm very glad to say the Princess and I made it up when we both attended the opening night of Scottish Ballet's lavish *Trainspotting 3*. Big Mags, I said, let's let bygones be bygones. Top up your Babycham and come *awa'* with me. We'll nip back to mine and act out *Abigail's Party*. I'll even let you be Alison Steadman. That convinced her!

We tried to creep out unnoticed, but unfortunately Darcey Bussell spotted us as she pirouetted across the stage with Jonny Lee Miller. It was kind of her, but ultimately foolish, to attempt to incorporate a curtsey into the already crowded choreography. The wee scone ended up toppling arse over elbow into the pit, landing on a furious first clarinet, with the giant needle sticking out of her arm shooting up, up in the air in slow motion like a javelin. We watched in horror as it rose above our heads and finally came into land on a snoozing Wayne Sleep at the back of the dress circle. I heard the evening never did get back on track after that.

We were glad to get home and I quickly rustled up a few things on sticks and a little impromptu cast. There was me and Big Mags, Antonio Banderas, Rupert Everett and Cherie Blair all sitting round in a circle clutching our scripts. Cherie had wanted an early night, but I banged on her bedroom door and said, sod Tony, let your hair down, woman, and, under my direction, she was perfect in the role of Sue. It still left us without a Laurence, but we lucked out when Gary Barlow returned from the Take That concert early… something about a row with Jason… and said he'd happily step up. Gary is such a nice, well-brought-up young man and he turned out to be surprisingly good at a northern accent. Princess Mags said she hadn't had so much fun since she and her sister dressed up as Hinge and Bracket and no one noticed the difference!

When I told the story to Susie Pluck, the less than impressive marketing manager at the Strathbogie Rep., she had the bright idea of a royal visit to boost the theatre's coffers. In fairness, I got her point. The reps have all gone, you see, there's only Strathbogie left. The rest have been consigned to the history books along with Carol Smillie, although her impeccable oral hygiene lives on. The council were slashing their budgets and June Whitfield and Eileen Atkins hadn't really done the business in *Kylie and Dannii – Sisters at War*, despite Dame Eileen bringing such depth to Dannii's character. Quite a remarkable feat when you stop and think about it.

Susie sounded so excited when she called to let me know that Holyrood Palace had confirmed a royal visit for July. Will and Kate are coming! We're saved, Kiki-Jean, we're saved! I'm ashamed to say my first thought was why couldn't it have been the Waltons, but I was truly happy for her. Well, two weeks later she's on the phone again, but it was like a different woman. I can't believe it, she sobbed, I'm absolutely devastated. Oh, petal, I'm so sorry, I said, don't say they've cancelled? No, she said, it's worse. They're sending Eddie and Sophie instead. We're doomed, Kiki-Jean, we're doomed! I felt for her, I really did, but I was able to reassure her that Eddie was once a theatre type himself, briefly, and certainly knew his way around a comedy of manners.

So, there we were, all lined up in our finery, hands outstretched, and what a delightful evening it turned out to be. Countess Sophie was so down to earth and chatted away, telling everyone how expensive her blouse was and laughing off Kit Harington's confusion that she was in *The Only Way is Essex*. No, we're from Wessex, she told him, only no one can find it on a map! Everyone laughed!

When it was my turn to speak to Eddie, he asked me if I had enjoyed *It's a Royal Knockout*? Well, what do you say? I managed to cobble something together about it being an important forerunner to the *Invictus Games* and deftly changed the subject. I've seen Charles Dance in his Speedos, I said, and if

You couldn't make it up… but she just did.

I live to see the Seven Wonders of the World, they will never be what he showed me that night. Well, next thing I know, the colour is draining from the Prince's face and he's asking if someone would kindly bring him a glass of water. I assured him it was only the balmy Perthshire air and the excitement of meeting me, but it didn't seem to help. Then I noticed the Artistic Director of the theatre, Denzell Cowan, looking daggers at me and before you know it he's giving our VIP a hefty shove down the line, saying, time is short, Your Highness, let's move on… may I introduce the fragrant Ms. Annie Lennox?

Denzell was a tad chilly with me for a while after that, but thankfully Strathbogie Rep. is made of girders. What would our town be without the theatre? And where does a young actor hone his skills without the bosom of a rep. company and an audience who don't get out much anymore? It's all *Hollyoaks* these days for the youngsters leaving drama school and you'll only learn bad habits there. Cuts, cuts, cuts! The poor bleeding arts! When will they learn it's we actors who are the real lifesavers? What would have happened to all those over-stressed, over-sexed dads in the '70s without half an hour of Felicity Kendal to look forward to each week? They'd have pegged it years ago.

Denzell feels very restricted in his choice of plays, as all they want round here are nice, safe Agatha Christies. No bad language, no leftie propaganda. No point, basically. Fortunately, he is constantly pushing the envelope, whatever *that* means, but he has his work cut out. The letters of complaint he receives from irate Strathbogie residents! I admire him for giving a platform to new writers, but last year's *Ruff and Muff in the Buff* led to the highest mortality rate in Greater Perthshire since 1897. I heard one old dear copped it the minute the curtain went up and sitting centre stage on a sun-lounger was a naked Joss Ackland, reading *The Times* and oiling his in-betweens. Personally, I loved it and I kicked myself for not bringing my opera glasses, but my neighbour, Bunion McTavish, wrote a stinging letter to Denzell about it. How could you humiliate a fine British actor in this way, she said? Denzell wrote back that Joss seemed to be having the time of his life and, *anyhoo*, how could someone who'd appeared in a Pet Shop Boys video ever be humiliated? I had it out with her over our rotary clothes dryers. You wouldn't be complaining if it was Eamonn Holmes, I said. Well, she couldn't answer that, could she?

She's the one who wrote to Delia Smith to try and have *West Side Story* shut down. She begged Delia to use her culinary clout to stop a production which she claimed glorified gang violence and would give the young hoodlums of Strathbogie ideas. As you can imagine, Delia was a mite confused, as she'd never even heard of Strathbogie and didn't see why the hell she should give a monkey's about its gang culture, until Bunny discovered she'd put the wrong letters in the wrong envelopes! Poor Denzell had been asking around everywhere for a recipe for Baked Alaska. You couldn't make it up!

You couldn't make it up... but she just did.

Shooting Stars

Mrs. McShoogle

I take the privacy of my guests very seriously; you have to in a small town like Strathbogie. You would not believe the curtain-twitching that goes on here in Condoleezza Crescent. How Cher lives with that level of intrusion day in, day out, I'll never know. We had the world's paparazzi camped out in the cul-de-sac when she stayed. All the glossy mags were here... *Woman's Own, Woman's Realm, Woman's Weekly*... rooting through my delphiniums at all hours of the day and night.

But Cher wasn't fazed. She just donned her towelling robe and shades and roller-skated past the lot of them with two fingers in the air. Then she'd whizz along the High Street and back to collect the latest copy of *Smash Hits*. She looks absolutely stunning for a woman in her nineties, but I've never known anyone take so long to get ready in the bathroom! Poor Stephen Fry was stood outside the door for hours, clutching his wee winkie and carefully cataloguing the contents of his toilet bag.

You couldn't make it up… but she just did.

My front lawn was ruined once that circus had left town, but I was very fortunate that the *Ground Force* team arrived shortly after and offered to re-lay it for me. Boy, they worked hard on that show and in such terrible weather. I always had a hot bath with Badedas waiting for them after a day's filming. Charlie Dimmock once shouted from the tub and asked if I would kindly bring her rubber duck. Lickety-split, I yelled and went into her room where I found it immediately, in her underwear drawer. It was the only thing in there. Well, you can imagine my shock when I walked into the bathroom and there were Charlie, Alan Titchmarsh and Tommy Walsh all in the tub together. Come on in, Tommy said, showing a shapely leg, you can help me get this cement off! The naughty slice! Tempting though it was, I said I really had to clean the downstairs lav. as Rex Harrison's aim had been far from perfect.

I've always been very comfortable with the human form in spite of my Highland upbringing. I did a spot of life modelling between jobs and I had no problem with nudity in a role if it was integral to the plot or Julie Andrews wasn't available. So why all the hullabaloo about the British remake of *Charlie's Angels*, *Wayne's WAGS*? It was as if the press had never seen a pistol hidden in bikini bottoms before.

At the height of the furore, David Frost had the temerity to ask me if it was just special effects. Oh, grow up, David, I said. I simply clenched the pistol in my buttocks in the privacy of my dressing room and when the director shouted, Action, I parted my cheeks, whipped it out and bam, bam, bam, the baddie's face down on the futon. Any police officer would have done the same. I could not understand what all the fuss was about. Every day on set I'd kept my purse and house keys squeezed between my buns. It helps to keep everything perky and you don't leave valuables lying around the dressing room when you're sharing with someone from *Emmerdale*.

You couldn't make it up… but she just did.

Of course, everyone remembers the famous photo taken when the original Charlie's Angels flew over to guest star in our little version. Talk about a bevy of beauties, there was Farrah Fawcett-Majors, Jaclyn Smith and Cheryl Ladd and alongside them there's me, Liz Smith and Christopher Biggins. Farrah was so gracious. She said she wasn't at all jealous that we seemed to be getting all the wolf whistles!

But what people don't see is the more serious side to an actor's work. When Brad and Angelina stayed with me on one of their humanitarian missions, they picked my brain about local war zones. Have you been to Aberfeldy, I said? They were very grateful for the tip and went the following day. I've never seen anything like it, Brad said, and Angelina nodded in agreement from the sofa where she was massaging Jennifer Aniston's feet. I warmed to them both immediately and learned so much, but I did have to ask them not to bang on about Syria when I was trying to watch *Countdown.* I encouraged

Angie to stand for President. Only you and George, Amal and the twins can save mankind now, I said, but she felt she had enough on her plate with *The National Enquirer* and the endless school run.

I am very proud to say I donated to Hillary Clinton's election campaign. I sent her some Body Shop bath salts and a copy of Stella Gonet's autobiography to help her relax. Ever the lady, Hillary somehow found time to write a warm thank you letter by return. She said the lavender bath salts were just the job and she found Stella's autobiography most interesting, if a tad short, and why was every chapter called *The House of Eliott*?

She then asked me for my thoughts about the thorny issue of Scottish independence. Where do you begin, Hillary, I said? I always find it a toughie to explain to my guests, but I try to give both sides of the argument. On the one hand, I say, it's nice to pop to the Lake District for the weekend without the need for a full body search.

You couldn't make it up… but she just did.

But on the other hand, Nicola Sturgeon is such a gobby wee dynamo you can't help but like her, can you? I call her The Midge as she really gets under your skin. She is the most incandescently beautiful woman I've ever met, and I've sat next to Sally Magnusson at a Motorhead concert. She has those come-to-bed eyes, cheekbones that would dwarf the average pair of shoulder blades and the daintiest wee feet this side of William Hague. I'd like to see her going solo. Do a Robbie, dearie. Or join up with Sandi Toksvig's girlies!

Last year, I was saddled with a block booking for the Tory party conference in Perth. I tried and tried to say no, but eventually Tory HQ sent Gyles Brandreth on a charm offensive. Think of it as charity, Gyles begged me, you would be doing it for posh people everywhere. I said, you may wear delightful pullovers, Gyles, but I don't need any lectures on charity work from the likes of you. I help out most Tuesday mornings at the Save the Royal

Bank of Scotland charity shop. But night after night of his never-ending anecdotes wore me down and I eventually gave in to that silver-plated tongue of his.

And what a pavlova it turned out to be. I had MI5 checking in the bins and under the beds and next thing I knew they were seizing my pogo stick! A particularly sour-faced young agent told me, we don't want Boris Johnson making an *eejit* of himself in front of the cameras, now do we, madam? And, before you know it, they had sent in the full gamut of forensic scientists in white suits. It was terrifying. I had no idea what they had found until I saw a line of them coming out of the downstairs loo holding the toilet brush at arm's length. Jerry Hall and I clung on to each other on the landing, thinking it had been poisoned or something, but after demanding an explanation from the chief security officer he said the area was now safe, but the offending article had been removed as it was so disgusting his officers refused to do their number twos in there…

You couldn't make it up… but she just did.

Sweet Jesus, I said, you lot would never make the SAS.

I was on the point of telling them to take their booking and shove it… to think I turned down John Barrowman for this… when all of a sudden a line of limos draws up beside my wheelie bins and out pops a very dishevelled-looking Coco the Clown. Well, slap my ass and call me Sally, I thought, the circus is in town, but as the poor specimen walked towards me I realised it was only Boris Johnson, closely followed by a young female companion called Sassy Fontana, Theresa and Philip May, and Andrea Leadsom with her ample luggage.

I have to say my heart melted when I saw Theresa and her hubby so very much in love. Philip was like Peppermint Patty, holding on to his wife's panties and blushing when she patted him on the head. She and I turned out to be kindred spirits. On the last day of the conference I served her kidneys at breakfast. These are Jeremy Corbyn's, I joked as I dished them up. You'd have heard the guffaw in Willesden Junction, and she tore into them after she'd finished hand-feeding Philip his Chocolate Shreddies. I complimented her on her outfit... I'd never dare to pair that tank top with those leather trousers, I said. A lot of people have said I channel Marilyn Monroe, she said. Do they, I said, taking a long look at her, I don't see it myself. Maybe a little Katie Hopkins?

Thankfully, the Prime Minister never came down to breakfast. I had warned him from the start, Boris Johnson, unless you can say something that is honest and decent and isn't just divisive, attention-seeking drivel, I don't want you to utter a word in my house between now and Friday. *[Boris Johnson's voice]* Why, I've never been so insulted in my life, he said. Oh, I think you have, I said. Theresa made a point of thanking me as we were sitting watching *The Silence of the Lambs* one evening. That silly man makes *me* look competent, she said! I had just swallowed a mouthful of banana milk and I laughed so much it went all over poor Andrea Leadsom, who happened to be walking past at the time. I'm frightfully sorry, I said, trying to wipe it off, but she was very forgiving. As a mother, she said, I always carry wet wipes and, as a mother, I have a clean change of clothes and, as a mother... Thankfully, Theresa interjected at this point and said we'd love to hang around and listen to you, Andie, but we really can't be arsed. I can't tell you the relief when they'd finally pissed off back to Westminster.

A Sky Full of Stars

You couldn't make it up... but she just did.

I always look forward to attending Scotland's very own *Academy Awards*, *The Tartan Tammies*. Every year Denzell manages to outdo himself, and this year's ceremony was no exception as a giant, blow-up Stephanie Beacham floated above us while we walked the red carpet. I thought she looked stunning, her big shoulder pads illuminated against the night sky, but I heard a few grumbles from Jane Asher, ahead of me in the queue, that *she* hadn't been given the great honour of becoming a barrage balloon. Be careful what you wish for, I thought a few minutes later, when the wind got up and she was bonked on the head by a free-floating and smirking Stephanie.

This year I was invited to the ceremony by J.K. Rowling, who is such fabulous company and so generous with that super-deluxe quadruple-platinum credit card of hers. The pair of us were seated at table number sixty-oatcake, which was some walk in heels... Ben Nevis would have been easier, J.K. said... but we had such a fun bunch at our table. I managed to wedge myself between Whoopi Goldberg and Ewan McGregor, and J.K. sat next to the patron saint of Scotland, Billy Connolly, and his gorgeous wife, Pamela Stephenson. That woman positively radiates a certain something spelt s-e-x and was kind enough to offer some marriage guidance to Sooty and Sue who shared a seat at the end of the table. We were all shocked to hear just how bad things were between them.

Just as we were topping up the Blue Nun, the lights began to dim and Denzell appeared looking very dapper in a satin onesie, leather cap and matching chains. Ladies and gentlemen, he said, please welcome your hosts for the 27th annual *Tartan Tammies*, the divine David Tennant and the handsome… Miss Hannah Gordon! I could not believe my ears. My dear friend, Hannah, in Strathbogie? And she wasn't staying with me? I was incredulous, I don't mind telling you, but even I got caught up in the frenzy when she was rolled onto stage wearing an R2-D2 costume! The woman looked hot! The crowd were on their feet, apart from Ewan McGregor, who remained seated and fumbling under his kilt in the chair beside me. Well, things are looking up, I thought, but next thing he had removed his underpants and was throwing them onto the stage yelling, love *ya*, Hannah Banana! Didn't we laugh! Ever modest, Hannah looked quite overcome at the reaction and flashed her buttons, rotated her head and whistled and bleeped some unintelligible but heartfelt robotic hogwash. She hasn't changed a bit, I thought!

The first half of the evening saw *Tartan Tammy* after *Tartan Tammy* going to the *crème de la crème* of Scottish talent. Best Scottish Drama went to the cast and crew of *Taggart* for the gazillionth year running, and then Best Scottish Actor went to Colin Firth of all people. Who knew? Apparently, the Academy couldn't think of any decent Scottish actors. David Tennant didn't look best pleased, as you can imagine, but *them's the breaks*, and thankfully Colin kept his speech short. Thank you most kindly for this honour. I may not be Scottish, but I once toured your beautiful, rain-soaked country in a Volkswagen Caravanette, all my love to Colin Farrell, that kind of thing...

Next up was Best Scottish Actress, which is always one of my favourites. It used to be a shoo-in for dear Molly Weir when she was alive, but now it's an open playing field, though they still nominate Molly for old times' sake. David went through the glittering nominations one by one and Ashley Jensen, Lindsay Duncan and Aled Jones each received a polite round of applause, but we all went wild when the last nomination was none other than Yoko Ono!

Yoko stayed with me last summer when she understudied for darling Maureen Lipman in the classic thriller *L'Amour et le Chien*. As it turned out she got to go on quite often as Maureen had other commitments... dentist appointments, Tupperware parties and such

… and one night when she went on a certain Michael Billington was in the audience. You can guess the rest! Yoko got a stonking review in *The Guardian* and poor Maureen was terribly upset as her Tupperware evening had been pants. All she'd bought was some useless jelly dish.

I waved to Yoko, who was nervously fiddling with her woggle, as Melanie Griffith walked on stage holding the winning envelope. Melanie looked a million dollars, but she didn't half witter on about the dinky Loch Ness Monster coasters she'd bought that day in a Poundshop. Thankfully, after a rather loud whisper of *haud yer wheesht, hen*, from R2-D2, she finally announced the winner and yet again the award was given posthumously to Molly. Well, the sense of disappointment in the room was palpable, but we are all professionals and duly applauded the sky with great gusto. I noticed that Ashley, Lindsay, Aled and Yoko were the first on their feet, which seemed incredibly generous until they started to walk briskly towards the exit, shaking their fists at poor Melanie, so I guess they weren't so happy for Molly after all.

The award was accepted by local spiritualist, Jeffro Lee Swingle. It was terribly moving as he told us that Molly was talking to him live from her cloud and she wanted to thank everyone for their kindness and to urge us to keep buying the *Rentaghost* DVDs as Vladimir, her beloved tortoise, needed the royalties. Then he said he had a bit of a scoop, as Molly had just confided that she was currently planning a comeback as she hoped to be reincarnated very soon! It's true what they say, actors never retire.

After all the excitement we settled down for the evening's entertainment and dear Billy Connolly took to the stage to read excerpts from *Titus Andronicus* in Gaelic. It's impossible to understand a word of the bloody thing in English, let alone Gaelic, so it was all bla*ch*, bla*ch,* bla*ch*, but Billy saved the day when he said, this is hoity-toity bullshit, isn't it, threw the script away and led us in a couple of choruses of his big hit, *In the Brownies*! The sight of Dame Judi Dench standing on her chair, skirt tucked into her knickers, and screaming, *we want you; we want you; we want you as a new recruit* is something I will never forget. Next up was Scotland's very own songbird, Moira Anderson, who sashayed on to stage in a sequinned jumpsuit and amazed us by singing all sixteen minutes of *French Kissin' in the USA*. After about ten minutes we were getting really worried, as all that sexy moaning had made her terribly breathless, but that voice… Kiri Te Kilmarnock, I call her. It's such a shame she didn't do more R&B, but I guess Fran and Anna got there first.

The final act was the legendary Lulu, my one-time flatmate, who belted out a sweet medley of *Donald Where's Your Troosers* and something called *Pour Some Sugar on Me*. I loved it, but the cloakroom attendant said to me afterwards, she wouldn't have won the Eurovision with that, would she? Well, everyone must have heard, as all you could hear were shrieks of laughter coming from the row of cubicles. No one could flush for laughing and a queue of ladies desperate for a dump started to form, until suddenly the door second from the end flew open and out stormed Lulu herself carrying an empty toilet roll tube and with a face like thunder! There's a lesson for us all there…

After the meal, if you can call it that… a deep-fried Mars bar and locally sourced *pommes frites* is not my idea of *using finest Scottish produce*… J.K. and I caught up with the multi-talented Alexander McCall Smith and his lovely wife, Lauren Bacall Smith, then returned to our table to find a rather dejected Whoopi toying with her pudding. This blancmange is rank, she said. I felt so sorry for her, coming all the way from Hollywood for a choice of that slop or prunes in custard, but by then we were all just desperate to get to the after-show party and there was still no sign of David and Hannah. I could picture Hannah backstage saying, let them wait; pearls before swine, darling; until finally David reappeared, looking very dapper in full Highland dress and then... talk about a collective intake of breath... a shiny spaceship was wheeled on stage and who should shuffle out, blinking under the startling glare of the lights, but E.T. It can't be Hannah, I screamed! But it was! What really gave it away was the exquisite Marc Jacobs handbag dangling from her extended, glowing finger. Phone home, my darlings, she teased the crowd, as she pretended to dial us in from a Trimphone. I'd never felt so proud of her, and Ewan said he could have done with those underpants now!

It's amazing how quickly we got used to E.T. with a lilting Morningside accent, but even Hannah couldn't liven up the next award for Best Radio Play. Frankly, who gives a flying fig? Anyone can say *[Radio 4 actor's voice] I am now walking into the bedroom; I am putting on my PJs; I am pouring from the Teasmade*. You just want to scream, buy a telly, don't you? Then

came Best Foreign Language Film, which
went to *Lorraine Kelly – A Life Well Lived*;
Best Original Music to Ed Sheeran with *He's
My Japanese Boy...* John Barry couldn't
believe his ears; and Best Hair and Make-Up
to Gloria, the Senior Stylist at the
Copacabana Hair Salon in Strathbogie High
Street. She only won because she's a close
chum of Denzell's partner, Wesley. It's who
you know in this business, as Nanette
Newman once said to me. Truly, Glo is a
hopeless hairdresser. She once mistook
Whitney Houston for Amy Winehouse and
gave her a dreadlocked beehive instead of a
shampoo and set. Not that it didn't suit her,
but she really should have checked first.

By the time David announced the award for
best on set meringues, the whole lovefest
was doing my head in, so I decided to catch
up on some correspondence. I was in the
middle of texting Sarah-Jessica Parker with a
photo of me with my arm around my dear
friend Kim Cattrall, when E.T. started to
read out the nominees for Best Newcomer.

You couldn't make it up… but she just did.

After a bit of faffing about, trying to put on her reading glasses over those ludicrously wide-set eyes, she opened the envelope and uttered the worst words I would ever hear… And the winner is… *[Pause]* Cyndi-Lou Redgrave-*McShoogle*!

It was like an out-of-body experience. What the hell was happening? Maurice had *married* the floosy? She's a *working* actress? *[Mad]* She's won a *Tartan Tammy*! *I'm* Mrs. McShoogle! *I'm* an acclaimed actress! They never gave *me* one! I felt violated and it didn't help when the crowd rose to their feet to cheer our so-called winner. I reached out to Sooty and said, help me please, but the wee critter was too busy practising his magic tricks for the party and just waved his little mitts at me. I remember thinking, even Sooty can't help me now, and that's not a line I ever thought I'd hear myself saying…

Mrs. McShoogle

Waiting for a Star to Fall

You couldn't make it up… but she just did.

Cyndi-Lou Redgrave-McShoogle! I looked around the table for support, but everyone seemed perfectly normal. Didn't they know? Why the hell were they clapping? I remember screaming, she's not an actress, she's a fireman's pole dancer, but everyone appeared to think I was just getting caught up in the excitement. You should have heard the roars when Mrs. Mutton-Dressed-as-Mutton stood up and waved to everyone while trying to look humble… except she's not *that* good an actress.

Then I saw him, my Maurice, looking tanned and toned in a lemon tuxedo, gazing up at her with such love and pride as she bent over and kissed him. And I mean a real, lingering *smackeroonie* on the lips. There were tongues. I swear there were tonsils! It was so distasteful with Macaulay Culkin present and, before I knew it, I had shouted, get a room, you whore! I must have hit rock bottom to use such language in front of Una Stubbs. But it was only when she started to wiggle her way towards the stage that I suddenly realised she had to walk right past our table to get there.

Well, I don't know what came over me, but before you could shout, *[Loudly]* your forehead's so stretched your eyebrows are vertical, I stuck out my slingback, said oops-a-double-daisy, and she fell headfirst into Gerard Butler's crotch. I know! I felt terrible, I really did, but there was no damage done other than a broken stiletto, and some cost to her modesty. What a gentleman that Gerard is. He took the sweetest selfie and put it on Twitter later. It went viral!

But the looks I was getting from around the room! The hostility was shocking and most undeserved. I tried to apologise most sincerely as she lay there, but oh no, Ms. Bung was having none of it. Whoopi had very kindly picked up all the items that had fallen out of her handbag... purse, comb, Methadone... but didn't get a word of thanks, as the original Loose Woman grabbed them, hoisted up her dress and hobbled her way towards the stage. To give her her due, she managed to read her acceptance speech with one half of her glasses smashed and I began to have a modicum of respect. Playing the victim seemed to be her best role to date, until she started the crocodile tears, bleating on about her husband… *[Loudly]* she means pimp, I shouted… mentor and best friend, Maurice McShoogle.

I wouldn't be half the actress I am without you, she said. You're only half an actress now, I screamed, as I began to enjoy myself, but the final straw came when she started to sing *My Love is Like a Red, Red Rose*. She didn't write that, I shouted, it was Pam Ayres, and next thing… well, I was like a woman possessed. I could hear my therapist Dr. Jekyll's voice saying, feel the fear, Jeannie, but in your case, for God's sake *don't* do it anyway, but I couldn't stop myself. I stood up, climbed onto our table and started to sing *Tell Me It's Not True* at the top of my voice. I assumed everyone would join in but the silence was deafening, apart from a series of protracted bottom burps from the direction of the *Last of the Summer Wine* table. Still, it was nice to see that every eye in the room went from the Mrs. McShoogle standing on stage to the Mrs. McShoogle standing on table sixty-two.

I was having a bit of bother remembering the rest of the lyrics… that Willy Russell is too clever for his own good sometimes… but I do remember Whoopi reaching over and stuffing leftover blancmange in my gob to try and shut me up, and Sooty hitting me with that pathetic magic wand of his. I think it hurt him more than it hurt me, to be honest. I never did reach that rousing final chorus, as Denzell suddenly appeared at our table and he wasn't looking his usual jovial self. It turned out he had instructed Nerys Hughes' bodyguard to remove me from the building, and next thing I know I'm being bundled over a rather muscular shoulder and marched towards the fire exit. *Me*, I shouted, what about *her*? Does she care that she's destroyed my life? Does she *Bublé*. That varmint stole my husband!

My words echoed round the room and, for a few seconds, I honestly believe the mood was turning in my favour. This is it, Jeannie, I thought, your big moment, and I was about to break into *Don't Cry for Me Argentina* when E.T., quite unnecessarily, shouted from the stage, your *ex*-husband, you fraud, the one you don't have a good word to say about! I was stunned, stunned at the effrontery, not to mention the betrayal… but I defy anyone to come up with a witty riposte, when the angelic Hannah Gordon is stood in front of you dressed as the world's most loveable alien.

Drat, I thought, as my dream of a new career in musical theatre began to look in doubt and I was unceremoniously carried out to the night's biggest ovation… which was at least some consolation. I waved and blew kisses to the crowd over the young man's shoulder, but once we'd left the auditorium,

I was manhandled through the kitchens, past Emily Bishop from *Corrie*, who was having a fly fag in the staff smoking area, and dumped in the overflow car park next to a pair of rather surprised-looking wood pigeons. I'd have expected more manners from a bodyguard of Nerys Hughes, but he just left me there, propped up against Stellan Skarsgård's Citroën Dolly.

For a moment the pigeons stared at me, then stared at each other in amazement, but I couldn't handle any more awkward silences for one evening, so I told them, don't worry, darlings, I'm in the business. There's no such thing as bad publicity! To this day, I'm not sure if they recognised me, but what a hullabaloo, I hear you say. Well, let me assure you, most sincerely, I am *full* of remorse, of course I am. She's a flash in the pan, a mere irritant, and it was a criminal waste of blancmange. But in my defence, darling Hugh Grant has done *much* worse and we all love him, don't we!

You couldn't make it up… but she just did.

When You Wish Upon a Star

After all the drama there was a bit of a hoo-ha in the press for a couple of days, but I was too busy trying to track down Maurice to put the record straight. I finally found him on Facebook and sent him a message saying I was terribly upset, and it had been a very trying evening for me seeing him with Miss *Fur Coat an' Nae Knickers*. I told him I'd always thought we were Rod Hull and Emu, can't live with you, can't live without you, and that one day we'd be together again.

He replied almost immediately and said it was certainly true he couldn't live *with* me, but he saw us more as Paul McCartney and Heather Mills, which seemed a teensy bit harsh. Then he finished by saying his lawyer was seeking an injunction to prevent me from contacting him or his poor wife ever again! Well, I must have read the message a dozen times, as I kept thinking, there has to be a hidden meaning in these words. Is he telling me he still loves me? That he wants me back? But eventually I concluded, probably not.

To add insult to injury, the following day I received an email from Denzell thanking me for my services to the theatre, whilst informing me he'd removed my name from the digs list. After all I've done for that bloody place! I emailed back and begged him to reconsider, giving Ian McKellen as a character reference and reminding him that without me he could kiss goodbye to Simon Callow's one-man show, but all I received was a three-line reply saying Ian McKellen's reference had been anything but flattering and he didn't need Simon Callow anyway as he'd booked Melvyn Bragg to give a fascinating talk on the history of the prawn cocktail. I don't think I've ever felt so let down in my life, and how Simon Callow will feel being upstaged by a prawn, I hate to think.

Denzell emailed again a few days later to tell me that he was now in receipt of even more damning evidence. Apparently, Sir Ian had bumped into Benedict Cumberbatch at the actors' laundromat, and Benedict told him some beastly nonsense about me being a kind of delusional fantasist declaring my unrequited love to a series of well-known actors! I was lost for words. I ask you, how could anyone *think* such a thing? And what's all this about unrequited? I demanded evidence, thank you very much, but he said he'd need a month to talk me through it all, quoting Champion, my former agent, as saying he'd dropped me years ago as I made Walter Mitty look like a Steady Eddie! I hit reply immediately and said there had been a simple misunderstanding. Champion must have meant it as a compliment, a testament to the vast range of roles in my repertoire. But I'm still awaiting the courtesy of an apology.

What hurts the most is that Denzell would take Sir Ian's word against my own. Dr. Jekyll tried to help me understand the situation better. Really, it's not so bad, he said, it's simply your word against Ian McKellen's. Well, not exactly, I said. Are you telling me there are *other* accusations, he said?

I don't know, I said, maybe a couple… it's all too painful to talk about. But you must talk, he said, I had this out with you in the sauna. You talk, I listen… you go home a new woman, I crawl home a broken vessel. Now, spit it out, how many accusations were there exactly? Oh really, it's only Hannah, Benedict and Sir Ian, I said, and Champion, if you count him, which I certainly don't. Well, that's not too bad, he said, not everyone has to like you, we're all made differently and… And Sooty and Keira, I continued, and Nigel and Barbra, Helena… Eddie and Sophie, Brad and Angie, Yoko, Whoopi, J.K. and Jane, Maureen, Moira and Gerard, Lord Lloyd Webber, Maurice, though he doesn't really mean it, Jerry, Lulu, dear Prunella… I never did get to finish, as I suddenly noticed the poor man was silently weeping, the tears rolling down his cheeks and dripping on to his bare chest.

I felt dreadful. Here I was droning on about my problems when he clearly had enough of his own. I'm so sorry, I said, please feel you can tell me anything... Ask anyone, I am very discreet. But the poor man just sat there unable to speak. Is it your wife, I gently probed? I never did take to her. Rumour has it she was hammering away with that Leonardo from the garage while you were in hospital donating your spleen to her mother.

I could tell I was helping when he started to dab his eyes gently with a tissue. No, it's not my marriage, he said, or at least it wasn't until now. I simply can't bear to listen to another word you say. You see, I never wanted to be a psychiatrist, I longed to be a hotel receptionist, but my parents said it wasn't a proper career. I still dream of handing out keys and telling people what time breakfast is served and... Why, that's beautiful, I interrupted, well done on sharing, thinking I'm buggered if I'll listen to any more of this self-indulgent bunk. You should share more often, I told him, maybe you could phone and make an appointment with yourself! At this point he started to laugh and cry at the same time, until he became quite hysterical. Good for you, I said, better out than in, as he took deep breaths into a barf bag. I'm so glad I was able to help. Same time next week?

One by one all my so-called friends in the business cancelled their bookings. They said it was nothing personal, they just didn't want to be associated with the likes of me. My final guests, Kirstie and Phil, left on Saturday morning and I admit to having a wee *greet* to myself as I waved her off in her silver Rolls-Royce with personalised number plates, and him on his rusty old tandem. They were filming that nice house programme of theirs with my neighbours, Bob and Betty Baxter. They're splitting up acrimoniously… Bob and Betty, not Kirstie and Phil, Heaven forbid! Everyone's talking about their terrible rows, so it's not entirely unexpected, but I'm sad for their chickens. I can't make out what they're fighting about, even when I stand on tippy-toes on their septic tank, so it should make for some good telly.

Mrs. McShoogle

The house is so quiet I find myself thinking the same things over and over. I ask myself *why*… why Helen Mirren? I could have been her if she'd only decided to become a nurse or something more suitable. I would have been a great Helen Mirren. Still could if the woman would only buy an Aga and a Top Loader and retire to the Cotswolds. I'm forever sending her details of idyllic cottages in Chipping Norton, not that I get any thanks for it.

I have found myself a fabulous new acting agent called Bullet Logan, who thinks I should play the hand that's dealt. If the public think you're deranged, then specialise in playing baddies! Bullet's currently serving time at Her Majesty's pleasure for fraud and crimes against colouring books, but he assures me he has the contacts to make mine the biggest comeback since Anthea Turner. I paid the deposit on the spot and have high hopes if I could only track him down. His mobile appears to be out of order, but I'm sure he's busy planning my big comeback!

You couldn't make it up… but she just did.

I can't even phone Maurice, as I'm told it would breach the terms of the restraining order. How silly is that, when there is so much we need to talk about? What I really should do is get myself down to Cats Protection to find another pretty little soulmate to share life's journey. I'm thinking I will call this one Sian Phillips, whether it's a boy or a girl. You're never alone with an animal, are you? They help make a house a home and they're such good listeners. Cats never judge you either… unless you're late in feeding them, sit in their favourite chair or look at them in the wrong way, of course.

Since Dr. Jekyll's enforced early retirement, I have been talking to my kindly, old-school GP, Dr. Finlay, and he has prescribed me some super-shiny anti-depressants and forbidden me from listening to any James Blunt records. Half my waiting room are here because of that bally man, he told me. Shocking, isn't it? No wonder the NHS is under such terrible strain. He also gave me a talking to about my lack of exercise, so I dug out my *Shape Up and Dance with Sheila Hancock* album last night. You'd be surprised how bendy that woman is, and I feel much better about myself today. I'm unable to stand up straight, but I'll skip the burpees next time around.

Dr. Finlay says he wants me to go for something called CBT. He said it will help me separate my thoughts and I must try and live in the here and now. Are you out of your tiny mind, I said? That's the *last* thing I need. I've spent my entire life trying to avoid the here and now! Bless him, he is such a clever man and has an almost encyclopaedic knowledge of the Carry Ons, but I could have done without the lecture about mixing up reality with fantasy. You say that as if it's a bad thing, I laughed, and thanked him for his concern, but assured him, don't worry about me, dearie, I'm happy! Happy, I tell you!

[Sings to herself as she stands up]

You couldn't make it up… but she just did.

La, la, la...

[She picks up her glass and swigs a mouthful of vino before walking over to the picture window]

[Fainter] La, la, la…

[Her singing tails off. A backdrop of mountains can be seen through the window. Silence follows as she stares out of the window for some time, before slowly turning and continuing.]

The mountains make for a nice view, but I can't look at them for long. I get too claustrophobic. They're a constant reminder that I'm still here. I'd leave in a flash for the right role, but, in the meantime, I must keep my creative juices flowing. People say to me, oh Jeannie, you're so full of crap, you'll believe your own stories one of these days, and I say, of course I do, darling! I'm an actress! How else would I get through the day? It's when I *stop* believing that I… *[Voice breaks]* panic.

Mrs. McShoogle

[Pause]

The nights are the worst. I lie there in the dark, willing myself to remember the bright lights, the famous faces, Hannah Banana… but my heart races and my head won't stop whirring. I feel like I'm going mad… as if none of it really happened.

[Pause, as she composes herself, then a faint laugh]

How ridiculous is that!

[She slowly turns to gaze out of the window again. Silence, as her two worlds collide…]

[Fade to dark]

Printed in Great Britain
by Amazon

62408577R00068